Grandad and Me

Written  ...on

Illustrat ...nde

Conscious Dreams
PUBLISHING

Grandad and Me

Copyright © 2022: Dorraine Robinson

First Printed in United Kingdom 2022

Published by Conscious Dreams Publishing

www.consciousdreamspublishing.com

@consciousdreamspublishing

Illustrated by Tosin Akinwande

Edited by Daniella Blechner

Typeset by Oksana Kosovan

ISBN: 978-1-915522-08-5

Dedication

To my grandad, thank you for being the best inspiration back then and still to this day.

Mum and Demi, thank you for all the times you listened and advised me through my book journey.

When we are together, we go for
long walks, just so we can talk.
He loves the outdoors.

My grandad is adventurous.

When we are together, we visit his allotment. We sow potatoes, carrots and peas. He never forgets to pick the weeds.

My grandad is skilful.

When we are together, he drops me to school. He always dresses really cool.

My grandad is stylish.

When we are together, we go for drives and talk about our past and present lives. He is my superhero.

My grandad is amazing!

When we are together, we buy sugary
cakes and crispy chicken bakes.
He always cleans my messy face.

My grandad is caring.

When we are together, we do chores
and complete my homework.
He calls it great teamwork.

My grandad is helpful.

When we are together,
we colour-in and paint pictures too.
He hangs them around the room.

My grandad is creative.

When we are together, we play dress-up using my Mum's makeup. He never gets the hump.

My grandad is playful.

When we are together,
we listen to music, dance and sing.
An oldies shing-ding is what he calls it.

My grandad is amusing.

When we are together, we go outside and I ride my bike. He always cheers me on from the side.

My grandad is encouraging.

When we are together,
we go to Brixton market.
He lets me fill the basket.

My grandad is generous.

When we are together, we cook creamy chicken soup. He says his recipe isn't in any cook book.

My grandad is talented.

After a day full of fun, we cuddle on the sofa. He is the best, absolutely better than the rest.

My grandad is loving.

Glossary

Absolutely	Totally or completely with no restrictions or limitations.
Adventurous	Full of excitement or willing to take risks or try new things.
Allotment	A plot of land for growing vegetables, fruits and flowers.
Amazing	Very impressive.
Amusing	Causing laughter and providing entertainment.
Considerate	Being polite and caring of others.
Creative	The ability to make new things or think of new ideas.
Encouraging	Being positive and giving support.
Generous	Happy to provide.

Helpful	Being useful and giving.
Loving	Feeling or showing great care.
Playful	Being full of fun and not taking things too seriously.
Shing-Ding	A big party to celebrate.
Skilful	Showing talent.
Sow	To plant seeds.
Stylish	Dressing fashionably, neat and tidy.
Teamwork	People working together to achieve a goal.
Talented	A gift of doing something very well.

About the Author

Dorraine Robinson was born and bred in southwest London. She has over 12 years of experience working with children and young people like yourself.

She is also the founder of Like Me For Me, a small business specialising in a range of children's black books and toys. She believes that it is so important for children all over the world to own books and toys that look like them because representation matters!

Unable to sleep one night, Dorraine decided that she wanted to personally add to the collection of books at Like Me For Me. She reached for her iPhone and started making notes for a children's picture book. What better story to tell than that of the loving relationship that she had growing up with her best friend and real-life superhero — her grandad? There started the journey of her debut book 'Grandad and Me'.

Follow Dorraine on Instagram at **@likemeforme_ldn**
Find out more about Like Me for Me at **www.likemeforme.co.uk**

My Grandad

In loving memory of Franklin Ward 1934–2007

Conscious Dreams
PUBLISHING

Transforming diverse writers
into successful published authors

www.consciousdreamspublishing.com

authors@consciousdreamspublishing.com

Let's connect

Lightning Source UK Ltd.
Milton Keynes UK
UKHW051539310822
408124UK00001B/1

9 781915 522085